Arthur Joseph Munby

Ann Morgan's Love

A Pedestrian Poem

Arthur Joseph Munby

Ann Morgan's Love
A Pedestrian Poem

ISBN/EAN: 9783337401368

Printed in Europe, USA, Canada, Australia, Japan

Cover: Foto ©Andreas Hilbeck / pixelio.de

More available books at **www.hansebooks.com**

ANN MORGAN'S LOVE

A PEDESTRIAN POEM

BY

ARTHUR MUNBY

A country lip hath oft the velvet touch :
Though she's no lady, she may please as much.

Post obitum vivam tecum, tecum requiescam,
Nec fiat melior sors mea sorte tuâ.

LONDON
REEVES AND TURNER
5 WELLINGTON STREET, STRAND
1896

If Woman be a child of circumstance,
  A creature of those habits and those rules
  That birth or breeding gives, and of the schools
And social arts whereby she may advance
This way or that, from merest ignorance :
  If these things be her makers, not her tools,
  Why then, we need not love her: none but fools
Would lose their hearts to accident and chance.

But if there be a Womanhood indeed,
  Which no defect of culture or of grace
Can maim or mar ; if that spontaneous seed
  Were found, sprung up in some unthought of place ;
Then, he who finds it, well might give his life
To foster such a sweetheart, such a wife.

CONTENTS

ANN MORGAN'S LOVE

BARE-ARM'D and buxom, rosy with her toil,
She hurried in, because the neighbours said
That some one call'd her.
                              At her cottage door
The doctor stood; who smiled, and said, "Well, Ann!
5 I knew you were a thorough servant-maid
Indoors, but *not* that you could work a-field!"

She dropp'd her curtsy; then, with injured look,
"Me work a-field?" she said; "Lor bless yo, Sir!
When Ah was joost a yoongling wench a-whoam,
10 Ah used to gather droppins on the roads
For father's 'lotment; an' fro' then to noo,
Theer inna mooch aboot a field or farm
But what Ah've doon it, an' can do it still!"

"Well," said the doctor, "I apologize:
15 They have not told me half your powers, Ann!
But, how are you? Nothing the matter, eh?"

A

"Naw, Sir," said Ann, "Ah's right enoogh! But Sir"—
She added, looking hard at him—"Sure lie,
Yo arena coom to gie me doctors' stooff?

20 *Ah* dunna want naw doctor!"

"No," said he :
"You're health itself; your face and your big arms
Speak volumes for you! But you know quite well
That when your Master went, I promised him
That I would come and see you now and then,

25 And tell him all about you."

"Aye," she said,
"Ah do remember : it was kind o' him,
An' kind o' yo to call, Sir. But ye see
Mah Master's foossy, been a gentleman :
Dear heart alive! He med have easy thowt

30 'At Ah was well—wi' sich a deal to do,
Joost what Ah like ; an' him a-coomin whoam
Three weeks temorrer!"

"Is he coming home
So soon? And can you tell me where he is?"
"Well Sir, they gie'd me t'naame ; but Ah forget—

35 Ah canna fraame to tell it. But Ah know
He's gone to foreign parts, a-pleasurin,
Across the sea ; they calls it *Italy*—
Ah do mind that."

"But *where*?" the doctor said ;

" For Italy's a *country*."

           " Is it, Sir ?

40 Well, theer's a paaper as he's wrote it on ;
Ah'll look ; but what, Ah canna find it noo—
Mah hands is black.   Sir, if yo wouldna mind—
But yo'd be shaamed, to speak wi' such as me
A-sellin fish—Ah'd give it yo to-night :
45 Ah've got to stand the market, at oor stall."

" Yes," said the doctor, laughing ; " be it so.
I know your stall ; and I have heard folks say
You are a famous fishwoman.   Perhaps
You'll let me have a penn'orth, just to try ? "

50 " Aye, Sir," said Ann ; "two penn'orth, if ye like !
An' charge ye nothin, neither.   Fish is dear,
To what they used to : it's the gentlefolks
Has fun' 'em oot ; an' all along o' that,
Us poor folks gets the worst on it."

           " Why, Ann,"

55 The doctor gravely said, " you're very sage :
Learned beyond your station !   Do you know
That this great problem of the rich and poor,
Which you have put succinctly into words,
Is full of deep complexity ? "

           Her eyes,

60 Her large blue eyes, grew wider as he spoke ;
She stared : then, seeing something in his face
That was not grave, she broke into a laugh,
And clapp'd her hard brown hands. " Dear heart alive ! "
She cried, " How you do best me wi' your talk !
65 Ah know'd no moor what yo was speakin on,
No, nor the baabe unborn ! You gentlefolk
Is all like that : my Master's joost the saame ;
He's at me wi' his dixonary words,
O' purpose to mak' fun o' me. But what !
70 Ah can best *yo*, wi' mah roogh coontry tongue,
As is a deal moor solid an' moor stright
Till them long words is, Sir ! "

                                  " That's right, fair Ann !
Your country tongue is better far for you,
And dearer to your Master, and to all
75 Who love the native English of their land.
But tell me—for I must have news of you—
What were you doing, when I came in here ?
They said you were at field work, out of doors."

" Eh, Ah was ony diggin, Sir ! Yo see
80 It's time o' year ; an' Ah were diggin in
What moock Ah'd gather'd. Ivery year i' Spring
Ah digs an' sets this garden ; doongs it well,

An' puts in taaters, cabbages, an' beans,
Onions, an' soochlike; an' again the sides,
85 Parsley, an' mint, or what the Master likes,
For garnish.   But Ah've welly doon it all ;
An' if we nobbut get a sup o' raan,
An' a good sun, why, things 'ull easy do
By when he cooms.   See ye ! this here's his room ;
90 Ah've sided it ; an' if it's poor and small,
An' joost a bricken floor an' nothink else,
Saam as mah kitchen, you can see yourself
As it's a parlour.   Sich a many books,
An' things to write, an' picturs on the walls,
95 An' real good chairs an' that !   Afoor he cooms,
Ah shall gaw doon upon my hands and knees,
An' scrub this floor, an' oil the furniture,
An' black the graate, an' sweep the chimley doon,
An' doost, an' clean the winder oot an' in,
100 An' set them pots o' flooers all a-row,
An' stick a posy on the taable theer,
An' silver, an' a napkin : all for him !
His parlour an' mah kitchen is as near
To one anoother, an' as mooch unlike,
105 As him an' me is."
                    With an honest smile
Of frank content and homely self-respect,
She spoke : and now the doctor look'd at her

More seriously, more sadly, than before.
Her handsome face, deep-bronzed by sun and wind ;
110 Her strong, bare, sinewy arms and rugged hands,
Blacken'd with labour ; and her peasant dress,
Rude, coarse in texture, yet most picturesque,
And suited to her station and her ways ;
All these, transfigured by that sentiment
115 Of lowly contrast to the man she served,
Grew dignified with beauty ; and herself
A noble working woman, not ashamed
Of what her work had made her.

                                 Not to her
Did he reveal emotion such as this :
120 He only said : " Well, Ann, you're very right,
To let your Master have such pretty things
And comforts, in this little room of yours,
As he's been used to. While he is away,
No doubt you use this parlour for yourself? "

125 " Me, Sir ? " cried Ann ; " *me* use the Master's room
An' him not in it ? That *would* be a thing !
Ah've nowt to do wi' parlours : when he's gone,
Ah shuts it oop, an' niver oppens it,
Ony for airin, till it's time to clean
130 An' side it, for his coomin back again.
The kitchen's *my* home, Sir ; an' always was,

An' always will be."

        " Well—and of its kind
You need not wish a better home than this,
This cottage-kitchen, opening on the lane.
135 You keep it clean : the oven and the range
Are black and bright—and that's your handiwork ;
You've scour'd the fender, and you've swept the hearth ;
The copper kettle shines like burnish'd gold ;
So do the tall brass candlesticks above ;
140 So does this ancient warming pan, that glows
Like sunshine on the wall ; and that old clock
Is a real treasure. But consider, Ann :
I know you like to take the lowest place,
As a rough homely servant ; yet, indeed,
145 Rough though you be, you are a woman still,
And not a man ; and everybody knows
That women are more delicate than men,
And more refined. Well then, you ought to learn
The love of books and pictures, music, flowers,
150 And all the dainty things that gentlemen
And ladies have about them ; you should share
The knowledge that your Master has ; the grace
Of his fair life should also brighten yours,
And make your service pleasant. Don't you see ? "

155 " Aye, Sir," said Ann, disdainfully, " Ah sees !

An' theer's a deal o' meanin in your talk,
Naw doot, if Ah could reckon what it is !
But dun yo reelly think, sich things as them
Has owt to do wi' *me* ?   Dear heart alive !
160 Me, all mah days a coontry servant-wench,
Bred on a farm, an' used to dirty work—
Scrubbin an' scourin, cleaning boots an' knives,
An' sich as that—what good is books to me,
Or picturs either, for sich work as mine ?
165 Well, Ah can read and write—thank God for that !
But Ah could clean a graate an' scrub a floor
As well as iver, if Ah lost it all
Or niver know'd my letters.   Books is good,
An' picturs too, for them as has no need
170 To soil their hands ; aye, an' for us an' all,
When work is ower'd.   That's my meanin, Sir ;
But they're naw good, to learn us what to do,
Nor how to get wer livin.   As for flooers
An' music—well, Ah sings a bit i' church ;
175 An' look ye theer, at all them flooers i' pots !
Ah've potted 'em, an' water'd 'em, an' all,
An' knows their naames : aye, women sich as me
Is tied to care for flooers ! "
                       With a blush
She paused, and said : " But Lor, Ah've spoke a deal,
180 An' stright on end !   It's clean above mah plaace

To talk like this to you, Sir ! Waw'd ha' thowt
Ah'd got the haselet for it ?"

      " Never mind,"
The doctor said, with his peculiar smile ;
" I don't object to haselet—not at all :
185 I like to hear a woman's arguments,
And see a sturdy servant-wench like you
Defend her calling. Speak your thoughts, my lass ;
I shall not be offended."

      " Well then, Sir,
Been as yo are that friendly, joost look here :
190 Yo talk o' women, an' yo please to say
As women is moor delicate till men :
It's fauseness, Sir—it's foolery ! Naw doot,
Laadies is nesh ; *Ah* could ha' tell'd ye that,
By oor Miss Marget, as could niver beer
195 To talk o' things what mun be talk'd aboot—
Let alone see 'em ; an' that poor Miss Day,
As kep the Margate lodgin-house, an' me
Her maid-of-all-work : couldna do a thing,
Her couldn't ; peel a taater, cook a chop,
200 Nor nothin : eh, Ah used to feel for her !
Ah used to think, it's better after all
To be a wench like me, an' bred to work,
Nor be a laady sich as her ; coom doon,
An' couldna do one job to help hersel,

205 For all her schoolin'! Naw, Sir; it's the use,
An' not the seck, as maks folks delicate:
Look at mah Master, then, an' look at me!
Wi' his fine fingers an' his dainty ways
He's like a laady; an' Ah often thinks
210 He *is* a laady, when Ah waits on him—
An' me a common mon."

                  "The more fool you,
Ann Morgan!" said the doctor, angrily:
"Your Master is as manly as the best,
For all his gentleness; and as for you,
215 *You* are not common; and you're not a man,
Nor like one. Why, the roughest part of you,
Your big red arms and your tremendous hands,
Are feminine, for all that: yes they are!"

Ann shook her head: "Theer's many women, Sir,
220 Has arms as good as mine, an' hands as hard;
If that's your meanin: but it inna hat;
An' what yo mean, the Lord o' mussy knows!
But Ah know one thing; if mah Master liked,
He's fit to sit at dinner wi' the Queen,
225 An' talk aboot Her Majesty; an' me
Not fit to hand the dishes to 'em—theer!
That's what mah Master is, by what Ah know;
An' that's what I are! Sir, yo talk'd o' things

To mak' mah service pleasant: bless your heart!
230 Service *is* pleasant, if you've got a plaace
As good as mine is, an' a mon to serve
As is that far above you—aye, an' yet
Can show hisself a Master joost as kind
As if he was a equal."

        "By the way,"
235 The doctor said (quite carelessly, it seem'd)
"Have you a sweetheart, Ann?"

        Her clear blue eyes
Look'd frankly at him; "Naw, Sir," she replied,
"Ah niver had a sweetheart—nobbut yan,
An him none neither, cause he didden know
240 'At Ah was fond on him."

        "Where is he now?"
"He's gone awaa, Sir."

        "But he's coming back
Three weeks to-morrow."

        "Sir!" the startled maid
Exclaim'd—and her wide-open eyes and mouth
Show'd blank astonishment—"Sir, you're mistook!
245 That is the day mah Master's coomin whoam."

"Quite so," the doctor said; "and I might add
Rem acu tetigisti; which implies
That you have hit the mark—and so have I.

You've got a sweetheart, Ann!   If that young man
250 Who does not know you love him, came again,
What would you do?"

           "Saam as Ah did afoor ;
An' that's joost nowt.   Ah wadna let him think
Ah liked him, if he didna care for me!"

"Right, right!   A modest woman's just reply.
255 But, if he *did* care for you, Ann—what then?"

"Eh, Sir!" she said, "Ah sure Ah canna tell ;
It's bad to think on!"

           " But you'll have to think,
And settle too : so, set about it now.
Ann, I have learnt your secret ; and I know
260 Who that young man is—though he's not so young
As one might wish ; well, you are fortunate :
Your sweetheart is—*your Master.*"

           " *What!*" she cried,
And started back ; and in her sunburnt face
The ruddy roses of her lips and cheeks
265 Grew pale beneath the brown ; she closed her eyes
And lean'd against the dresser ; and her hands
Fell forward, helpless.   Yet she did not faint ;
He knew she would not : such a girl as this,
Strong, rustic, sensible—whate'er she feels,

270 Is no adept at fainting.   Presently
She roused herself, and stood erect again,
And look'd at him with shy and timorous eyes,
As in a low uncertain voice she said
"Sir, yo'll excuse me : *do the Master know ?*"

275 "No," said the doctor ; "I am sure of that ;
He does not know.   And I too did not know,
When I came here : Ann, you betray'd yourself !
Your earnest words convinced me that you felt
More than a woman should, for any man
280 To whom she is a servant.   But with you
The case is different, now.   You understand
That I came down to see you here to-day,
Because your Master ask'd me, as his friend,
To do so, and to tell you quietly
285 About his feelings, and to find out yours,
And see if you could love him : if you can,
I know he means to marry you."
                           Those words,
"To see if you could love him," oh, how strange
They seem'd, to her who loved him all along !
290 Well, but they show'd he had not found it out ;
And that was something.   "Sir," she slowly said,
With downcast eyes and hesitating words—
And her bronzed face grew redder than her hands

As she went on—"if he say that to me,
295 Wativer shall Ah do ?   It's like enoogh
As Ah can love him ; for Ah canna beer
To think o' leavin, an' anoother plaace,
An' not to be his servant ; but his *wife*—
Eh, that's so different !   It 'ud be disgraace,
300 A mon like him to wed a wench like me ! "

" *He* does not think so," said the candid friend ;
"And, since I am no relative of his,
I need not think so neither.   But you see
You will no longer be the same rough Ann
305 That you are now ; no, that would never do !
Your simple cotton frock, your servant's cap,
Your kitchen apron, all will disappear ;
For he will change you, and you will be changed.
You will give up your common work and ways ;
310 You'll make your hands and arms as smooth and white
As any lady's ; and you'll go to school—
Yes, Ann, you'll go to school, and there be taught
To love the things I spoke of.   Most of all,
You must forget your homely country tongue,
315 And be grammatical, and learn to speak
In pretty phrases and in fine long words,
Like folk who live in parlours.   That is hard ;
But, since your sweetheart is a gentleman,

You must become a lady.   So, prepare !
320 Or be for ever what you are—a drudge."

That was plain speaking ; but the candid friend
Perhaps had motives ; did not quite approve
So strange a *mésalliance ;* thought to rouse
Ann's rustic self against her misplaced love,
325 By showing her the issue ; making clear
That such a marriage could but take away
All that she cared for; all her humble life,
And hope of service ; could not but degrade
The man she loved, and do no good to her.
330 " If she feels this," the wily doctor thought,
" Then, since her nature, rugged though it be,
Is noble, and her maiden heart is pure,
She has the woman's gift, self-sacrifice,
And she will use it : she will give him up
335 For his own sake, and suffer all alone."

Ah well—he overreach'd himself.   His words,
Simple enough, yet like a foreign speech
To her rude ears, confused her as they came ;
But listening, she painfully pieced out
340 Their meaning and their drift ; and all the while
Her mind grew clearer, and her courage rose ;
Till, when he ceased, she had no fear at all,

No doubt, no hesitation.   " Sir," she said
Slowly, and with a grave respectful air,
345 "Ah thank yo for your tellins ; an' at last
Ah've coom to understand 'em.   Yo ha' said
The Master thinks o' me to be his wife,
An' means to offer : him a gentleman,
An' me a laabourer's dowter !   To be sure,
350 That is a honour for to mak' one proud ;
But not to chaange wat niver can be chaanged.
Ah canna chaange mah natur an' mah ways ;
Ah've lived like this for five an' twenty year,
An' likes it ; an' Ah's fit for nothink else,
355 Nor dunna want to be.   An' if Ah've dar'd
To look above me for a sweetheart, Sir,
That's noan presumptious ; cause Ah niver thowt,
Nor niver wish'd, to be na'moor to him
Till what I are.   Ah'd liefer by a deal
360 Be joost his servant, nor to be a wife
To onny oother mon.   An' as for schule—
To learn fine talk an' little fidfad things,
Why, its ridic'lous !   Me, at twenty-five,
To gan a-schulin amoong laadies—nay,
365 It shanna be.   Saw this is wat Ah says :
Yo give mah duty to the Master, Sir,
An' tell him, if he can demean hissel
To sich as me, as shouldna look that high,

Ah winna be contrary ; but Ah think
370 He'd better let ma' be.   Yo knaw yourself,
Ah wouldna shaame him for a hunderd poond
An' moor till that : but be yo sure o' this—
Ah winna be a laady ! "

     " Good," said he ;
" I'll tell him what you say.   And you are wise,
375 To take the matter calmly.   Now, Goodbye ! "
And as he went, he thought " The thing is safe ;
He cannot marry her."

     " Calmly," he said :
He little knew her !   Wenches such as she,
Rough and untaught, but honest and sincere,
380 Have sometimes depths of feeling, more profound
Than slighter maidens know of ; they have hearts
That glory in their lowliness ; and love
That asks for nothing, will have no reward,
Except the right to serve.

     When he was gone,
385 That wily friend, she dropp'd into a chair,
And laid her face upon her strong brown arms,
And cried a little ; then, she sat upright,
And threw her kitchen apron o'er her head,
And thought awhile.   " Aye, Ah ha' doon quite right,"
390 She thought, " an' Ah mun stick to it.   At last,
He'll knaw wat's in me : let him think o' that,

          B

An' think o' me as says it ! Ah could beer,
Ah know Ah could, to see him wed i' church
To soom fine laady, if he wanted her ;
395 He owt to have a laady to his wife,
Aye, an' a grand un : but Ah couldna beer
Him to be tired o' *me*. Na' moor he need !
For in mah kitchen Ah could serve him still,
An' her's no call to knaw. But that's not fair ;
400 It's underhanded ; it 'ud niver do.
Well then ; if he can fraame to think o' me,
An' tak' me what I are, an' mak' naw fooss,
Ah'll be his servant an' his wife an' all—
Aye, bawth tegither. It's a easy thing
405 For sich as me ; my own poor folks 'ull knaw
'At Ah'm a honest woman ; as for him
An' his fine friends, why, let 'em coom an' gan,
Like they do noo, an' reckon nowt o' me !
Ah shall be t'saam, in iverything but yan,
410 An' that's mah weddin ring. Aye, *that*'ll do—
An' a good job, Ah've sattled it ! "

                                       She rose,
And went at once about her daily work ;
Active as ever ; happy in the thought
Of such a lifelong servitude for love,
415 And such a lowly wifehood.

                                           Silently

The days went by ; she scrubb'd and swill'd and scour'd,
And swept the house ; and most of all, she clean'd
The Master's parlour ; with her rustic taste
Adorning it for him.   At last, one day
420 A letter—rare experience ! came to her ;
Address'd, *Ann Morgan.*   It was simply this :—
" Ann, I am coming by the evening train ;
Have dinner ready."   That was all : no love,
No hint of his affection.   She was glad ;
425 For she had wish'd that nothing should be said
Till all was said.   She kept the letter, though ;
And hid it in her Bible.

               When he came,
She gave him just a servant's welcome home ;
The simple curtsy and the sober smile
430 That he had always had : although indeed
The roses in her cheeks were ruddier,
And her blue eyes no longer look'd at him
So frankly as before.   But she went out
And did her duty ; brought the luggage in,
435 Up to his room ; and, when she thought it time,
Knock'd there, and said " Your dinner's ready, Sir."
    Yes, he must dine !   And truly, from of old
Ann knew the worth of dining ; she herself
Enjoy'd her noonday bacon and her beer ;
440 And oh, what dinner is, to gentlefolks !

A sacrament, an outward visible sign
Of social grace, and wit, and *badinage*.
Dinner, great centre of our human life,
Prime mover of the spirit and the soul,
445 Majestic Power ! If thou art not benign,
All hope may vanish, and all projects fail :
And Love's fail first ; for who would e'er propose,
Or who accept, unwarranted by thee ?
Therefore, he dined ; and she behind his chair
450 Stood quietly, or moved about the room
Bearing the dishes : not a word was said ;
And when the meal was over, silently
She fill'd her tray, and laden, disappear'd.
But when the bell had rung for prayers, and prayers
455 Were ended, as she glided to the door,
He call'd her : " Ann, I wish to speak to you."
She stopp'd, turn'd pale, and trembled as she stood :
" Yes, Sir ? "
                    " You saw the doctor ? "
                                        " Yes, Sir."
                                                  "And
He told you all my message ? "
                                        " Yes, Sir."
                                                  " Well,
460 What do you think of it ? "
                                        " Aw Sir," she said,

" Ah dunno what to think, nor what to say !
The doctor tell'd me yo'd explain it all—
But me, Ah darna reckon as it's true."
" Why not ? "

          " How *can* yo ax me that, Sir ? Think—
465 Think o' the difference ! "

                    " The difference !
To me, and those who think as I do, Ann,
All that is in your favour.   Now, look here :
You've served me, and you've work'd both well and hard,
Five years and more ; and that is quite enough
470 To know you by.   I always have admired
Your beauty, and your stature, and your strength ;
Your skill in labour, and your willingness
To do my bidding ; but that is not all :
No, I have watch'd you in your work and ways
475 Among your fellowservants ; and have seen
How you have help'd your parents and your kin
Out of your wages.   Other maids like you
Have done as much ; but that too is not all :
You are no common servant, Ann ; I see
480 In you, a nature and a character
Above the working women of your class,
Aye, and above my own class.   For indeed
The ladies fritter half their life away
In polishing the other half; but you,

485 Who have no polish, and have had no chance
To learn accomplishments, you stand here now
Just as God made you : simple, honest, pure ;
Healthy and strong ; and full of sterling sense,
And gentleness, and meek humility,
490 And earnestness in work. No higher praise
A man could give a woman ; be she drudge,
Or be she duchess. As for other things
That I think little, and the world thinks much ;
They can be alter'd, better'd, beautified :
495 You are untaught—but you have brains to learn ;
And you are rough with labour—but anon
Labour will cease ; and then, your comeliness
Will shine out clear. But mind you, for myself,
I like your red arms and your harden'd hands
500 Far better than a lady's. They are signs
Of duty done unselfishly and well ;
But hers are signs of nothing, save vain ease,
And sleek prosperity. And now," said he,
Rising, and holding out his hand to her,
505 "Ann, will you be my wife ? I did not know
Till now, that your devotion to myself
Was more than service ; and 'tis much, to think
You care for me as I too care for you.—
You understand what I have said, I hope ? "
510   For she stood silent ; looking doubtfully

With moisten'd eyes ; nor would she take his hand—
Not yet : he would contrast his own with hers,
And the mere touch might shock him.   But to think
Of all the many things she had to say,
515 And had already said within her heart
And even to the doctor !   And yet now,
In presence of her master and her fate,
She could not say them.

          Seeing her distress,
" Ann, dear," he said, " your silence gives consent ;
520 Is it not so ? "

          She started and she blush'd,
And her moist eyes ran over : what was this ?
No man like him had ever call'd her *Dear*—
And now, he did so, who was more to her
Than all the others !

          " Master," she replied,
525 " I are your servant now, an' nothink else ;
An' Ah could wish to be your servant still
For all my life, if yo would let me, Sir :
Ah ax na' moor.   As for your pretty ways
An' schulin—nay, Ah'm got too owd for it,
530 Too roogh an' ignorant ; Ah canna chaange ;
I arena fit to be your wife at all,
If Ah mun be what yo are ; that's the trewth ! "

He smiled, to see her sudden vehemence ;
And yet, it raised his pity and his love
535 Higher than ever ; and he softly said
　　"Well, you can settle these things by and bye,
　　When we are married.　Surely, you would like
　　To leave off cleaning boots and blacking grates,
　　And scrubbing floors, and to sit down with me
540 Here, or in that old parlour at the Grange,
　　And be at leisure ?　You will read nice books,
　　And I shall tell you all you wish to know,
　　And make you happy in a way quite new,
　　And yet quite simple ; so you need not fear."

545 "Sir," she exclaim'd, in sadness and surprise,
　　"Yo canna reelly think as sich a life
　　'Ud do for *me* ?　Ah'd like to read nice books,
　　An' Ah could learn a deal, Ah'm sure o' that,
　　If yo was teacher ; but to sit oop here,
550 An' not do nothing for mysel nor yo,
　　Ah couldna beer it, Sir !　A wench like me
　　Mun show her love by doin all her can
　　For him as loves her : Ah shall work for yo,
　　Wife or no wife, in service like I are,
555 While I ha' hands to work with—*that* Ah shall !"

　　He smiled again ; as if it were a jest,
　　Her way of loving : but he only said

"Ann, we will talk of that, another time :
Whatever happens, and whate'er you do,
560 I've ask'd you, and you have not said me nay—
So you shall be my wife. Now then, come here,
And take my hand."

            Reluctant and confused,
She gave her hand ; he took it, held it out
Toward the light, and stroked it, up and down
565 The stiffen'd fingers and the callous palm,
As if he loved it ; saying to himself
" It is a shapely and a noble hand !
Large, and of course disfigured and deform'd
By labour ; but, when once the labour's done,
570 It may become a lady's."

                "Niver, Sir !"
Cried Ann, who heard him with astonishment ;
" Mah hands shall always be what they are now,
An' so shall Ah be ! Ah'd be shaamed indeed,
To have a laady's hand ! "

             Again he smiled—
575 Smiled and said nothing, the provoking man !
But raised her ruddy fingers to his lips,
And kiss'd them like a courtier. With a start
Of wonder and of gratitude, she blush'd,
And drew her hand away ; and he turn'd round,
580 Saying, "Fair Ann, I've paid my footing here,

And now I claim your lips : they are not spoilt
By duty, like your hands ; work has not marr'd
Their freshness and their fragrance ! "

It was true ;
And so he found it, having in his arms
585 The maiden whom he loved.

" Now go," he said ;
" Go quick to rest ; and when to-morrow comes,
Write to your mother.   In a fortnight's time,
You'll have to name the day."

So that was all
Of courtship, 'twixt the Master and the maid.
590 They knew each other ; in the selfsame house,
So near and yet so distant, each had lived
Observant of the other.   From above
He noticed her : her face had struck him first ;
A quiet face, serenely beautiful
595 In feature and expression ; ladylike
In outline ; but in texture and in hue
" Subdued to what she work'd in " ; like herself,
A medley strange of rustic and refined.
It was a peasant's face, undoubtedly :
600 The fair blue eyes show'd nothing from within
That was not native : no imported grace,
Nor knowledge, nor experience ; no fine art
Of how and when to open or to close

Her fascinating eyelids.   No fine art
605 Had bronzed the rural roses of her cheeks,
Nor touch'd her innocent mouth, whose soft red lips
Were sweet and wholesome as the udder'd kine
That she had milk'd and tended.   But in her
Were traits above her calling ; qualities
610 Which, rightly train'd by duty or by love,
Might make her life heroic.   She was tall,
And statuesque in pose and character :
A servantmaid, and yet not frivolous,
Nor vain, nor vulgar ; caring not a whit
615 To ape her betters ; rather, standing by
In proud humility, to let them see
How different she was from their ladyships
In dress and manner ; seeming so to say
" This is my station, and the work I do ;
620 I'm not ashamed to be a servant, Ma'am ! "

Such was the vision that he had of her,
De haut en bas ; and all her deeds and ways
Had verified his fancy.   He meanwhile
Among the ladies of his rank and age
625 Sought vainly for a heroine, to match
His unsuspecting servant.   Surely they,
Advantaged by their training and their birth,
Must be superior to a girl like this !

But she, obscure and humble though she were,
630 Was yet original : and what were they ?
Mere imitations, commonplace and cheap,
Of something other than themselves.　He saw
Their life, their knowledge, their accomplishments,
Their very pastimes, were not of their own,
635 But changed and fashion'd by each fleeting hour
Of popular applause.　If they had sense,
And merit, and a purpose, they grew vain,
Presumptuous, or eccentric ; and if not—
Why, that was worse than t' other !

　　　　　　　　　　　　So he turn'd
640 And look'd at her, who had no part nor lot
In ladyhood, nor in society :
She had no knowledge ; she could never tell
What books to read, what pictures to admire,
Nor what opinions ; no, nor where to go,
645 Beyond her native county.　What she had
Was small indeed ; but then, it was her own :
She had in her the making and the mould
Of better things than fashion, or than fame.
And so he look'd and look'd, and from her face
650 Sketch'd out a future for himself and her,
Till contemplation ripen'd into love.

　　And what did she do ?　Gazing from below,

Far off, and in so mean a standing place,
How came she thus to love him ? That she did
655 A thing so bold and dangerous, was due
To finer feelings and a better taste
Than her rude class affords. She did not care
For Jack or Tom, the jester and the clown,
Who follow'd her, and woo'd her company
660 Against her will ; she did not want a mate
Of her own sort, unlearned like herself,
Incompetent to guide : she wanted *him,*
Because he look'd so clever and so kind,
And was so much above her, that he seem'd
665 All that the white man to the savage seems,
·All that the savage to his faithful dog.
She wanted love, and leadership, and light,
That she might share, as favour'd pupils share
The studies of their teacher ; and of all
670 She yearn'd for, this she yearn'd for most of all—
To be his servant. Thus she would repay,
By her own labour, frankly and at ease,
The care, the guidance, the companionship,
Which he, she thought, could give her ; and escape
675 That which she chiefly dreaded : the belief
His friends would have, that such a love as hers
Was merely degradation and disgrace
To one like him ; for, if they did not know

She loved him, they could never blame her love.
680   She had no theories ; the very word
Was meaningless to her ; and all her thoughts
Were fluid and unshaped ; she had no skill
To shape them, and no words to put them in.
But they were strong ; for she had strength of will,
685 And these were instincts : instincts of a soul
That knows its mate, but knows not how it knows.

    So those two loved each other, and were wed ;
The Master and the servant.   All her kin,
But none of his, came thither to that sight ;
690 And thus their life began.   No outward change ;
No sign of marriage, save her wedding ring ;
For so she wish'd.   He only took to him
A rough hardhanded homely kitchenwench
To be his mated wife ; and gain'd thereby
695 The hatred of his kinsfolk, and the scorn
Of all those ladies whom he might have woo'd
And might have wedded.   What could make amends
For such disastrous consequence ?   Why, Love !
Love under new conditions : the success
700 Of this untried experiment of his.
    For, he would show them what a woman is,
Simply as woman : how she can be raised,
By virtue of her very womanhood,

For yo to reckon what to do wi' me,
Been as I are your wife."

        " Exactly so,"

805 Said he ; " *rem acu*, as the doctor says—
You've hit it."

        " Well then, if so be it's that,
Yo've nowt to reckon, Sir ! Yo've took me oop,
A wench as always work'd for yo for love
Better till waages ; an' yo've gi'en me right
810 To sit beside ye, an' to read to ye,
An' hear ye tell a many hunderd things
As niver cooms into sich heads as mine,
For want o' knowin : that's what yo ha' doon ;
An' thank ye for it ! But yo canna think
815 All *that* could mak' me different : Bless your heart !
Why, onny menseful woman sich as me
'Ud feel like Ah do, what a thing it is
To maate hersel wi' sich a mon as yo.
But wat, Ah've doon it, an' Ah sticks to it,
820 An' thankful too. Eh, Master ! dunna think
As Ah forget what yo ha' bin to me,
An' always will be ! But Ah says again,
Ah mun joost love ye i' my own poor way,
An' not i' your way. Ah can be a wife,
825 But not a equal—niver ! "

        He look'd grave

He kiss'd her fondly, but he still look'd grave,
And answer'd nothing.   And they both went home.

She had her way; of course she had her way.
How could he keep her in his own large house,
830 Drest as a servant, waiting on his guests,
Yet known to be his wife ?   But, after all,
How noble, how unselfish, her resolve !
What other woman in a class like hers
Would do as she did ?   Married to a man
835 So much above her ; raised in name and rank
To his own level ; he himself prepared
To give her all the pleasures and the toys
That women care for, and the envied style
Of *lady*—envied most of all by those
840 Her former fellows, on whose humble toils
She might look down, herself attended now
By other servants ; all this pageantry
Was hers by right ; but she would none of it ;
Disdainfully, with philosophic scorn,
845 She put it wholly from her : and for what ?
Why, for her husband and her nobler self.
     Should she forsake her class, and seem to say
She was no longer one of them ?   Not she !
She knew their labours and their homely life,
850 And knew no other : she would be to him

Companion ?   Yes, if he would make her one ;
But most of all, a minister for love,
As she had been for wages.   No one else
Could so secure the comfort of his home
855 And keep his dwelling cleanly ; no one else
Knew all his habits and his daily wants
As she did ; should she leave to other hands
All that her own hands had been wont to do
So long and so intently ?   Could she bear
860 A stranger housemaid or an alien cook,
Another maid of all work like herself,
To come between her and her proper place,
And do her duties, while she left her sphere
To play at prettiness, and entertain
865 Folk who despised her ?   No ! her honest heart
Revolts at such a thought, and doubly warms
Toward the coarse apron and the cotton frock
And servant's cap, that she had always worn,
And would wear, will he nill he, to the end.
870 Not even he, the Master whom she loved,
Should keep her longer from that lowly work
For which God made her.   *That* was her resolve.

     And he ?   He listen'd with a varying mind
To these her arguments : not stated thus,
875 Oh no ! but with affectionate respect,

And meek determination, day by day
Impress'd on him, in many an antique phrase
Of peasant utterance : " Thee bist so gain,"
She fondly said, *tutoyant* him for once,
880 " Sure lie, thee's catch'd mah meanin ! "

                                        So he had ;

He tried her practice by his theories,
And silently confess'd that she was right.
How such a husband could with such a wife
Live openly, in permanence and peace—
885 That was the problem : they so much unlike,
And yet so wholly passionately one
In heart and feeling ; not a single cloud
To dim the humble heaven of their love.
He put the case, and thus he answer'd it :
890 Around him were accumulated stores
Of art and learning ; pictures, porcelain, books ;
The heritage of ages : and to her
All these were unintelligible things,
Which she could keep in order, dust, and clean,
895 But scarcely even wish to understand.
She did now wish it, though ; she dearly long'd
To understand her Master, and improve
Her simple self ; nor could his ample stores,
And all the circle of his wellbred friends,
900 Even were they willing, help toward that result

So much as he could, singly.   That was clear,
Because her only stimulus was her love.
And after all, what were such things as these
That he could give her—money, pleasure, power,
905 And what the fools call culture—what were these,
Compared with her one gift, self-sacrifice
That would not be refused ?   Self-sacrifice
Means Love ; and Love has no competitor,
Being supreme of all things ; absolute,
910 Immortal, self-existent, uncreate.

Ah yes !   All that is proper—in a creed ;
But should such stately epithets as those
Be lavish'd on a woman of the herd
And her poor fatuous passion ?   He was sure
915 The world would call it fatuous ; and would ask
What credit is it, to a drudge like her,
That she prefers her drudgery, and declines
To be what she has sense enough to know
She never can be ?   Such an estimate
920 Was false ; he knew it ; but he also knew
They did not know her, and they never would.
   Then, why regard such judges ?   Prejudiced,
Incompetent, unable to decide
For lack of evidence !   But, he himself—
925 Was he unprejudiced, and competent ?

Was he not blinded, as most lovers are,
By her mere beauty, and disposed by it
To think too well of her capacity
For learning, and her willingness to learn ?
930 But then, he had his evidence of that,
In what she had learnt ; and to test her love
By her intelligence, by her degree
Of understanding and companionship,
Were cruel, and irrelevant.   For her
935 He ought to do what she had done for him ;
And Conscience gave the word : self-sacrifice.

     What was she doing, when the doctor came
And saw and talk'd with her ?   She had been sent
Beforehand, to make ready in the house
940 And garden, for his group of thoughtful friends
Who spent with him the spring and summer there,
Rambling by day, and far into the night
Talking of things as much beyond the scope
Of her small outlook, as their full bright lives
945 Were loftier than so poor a life as hers.
She *did* make ready ; even the housekeeper
Confess'd reluctantly, yet still confess'd,
That Ann had done what she was told to do
As well as could be, for a wench like her.
950 Each year she earn'd her strict superior's praise
For work like this ; and, living by herself—

A staid and trusted damsel, left alone
To do the rougher labour, and prepare
For that high dame, whose educated skill
955 Would mould her awkward efforts into forms
Fit for the Master—she had leave from him
To see her own acquaintance in the town
Freely, and help them at their little trade.
For they sold fish ; and she behind the stall
960 Would stand on market days, with civil tongue
And modest smile attracting customers :
Youths of the place, uncomfortably shy,
Who dipp'd their morsels in the vinegar,
And ate, and came again, to look at her.
965 Such was her life ; and every year till now
She had been happy, when the Master came,
Waiting on him and on his visitors ;
And happier, when no visitors were there,
Waiting on him alone.   Contract the scene :
970 Omit the friends, remove the housekeeper,
And change the place of dwelling : was not that
A fair solution—a superlative ?
Peace for himself, and paradise for Ann !

There is a village in the Bradwyn Hills,
975 That looks on Albany, and often sees
The broad moon shining over Elsley Mere.

There was she born ; and there, each man and maid
Knew who she was ; and many too had seen
Her wedding with the Master.   " Ann," he said,
980 " How would you like to live at Burlinghope ? "

" Eh ! " she replied, and in her calm blue eyes
A soft light gleam'd, and as her manner was
She threw her arms abroad in ecstasy—
" Eh, Master, that 'ud be the very thing !
985 At least, if yo could like it.   Bless your heart !
Why, Ah can be myself, at Burlinhope ;
Ah canna be nowt else.   A pretty thing,
For me to goo on different, an' pertend
To be a laady, when oor Jim lives theer,
990 An' Polly, an' the rest on 'em !   Ah think "—
She added, with a meditative look—
" 'At Ah could help 'em wi' the stall, a bit,
An' stand the market, like Ah used to do,
If yo would let me."
                                        With a hearty laugh
995 He answer'd " Oh yes ! I should like it well,
To see you standing there behind your stall,
In your hood bonnet and your cotton frock
And clean white apron, dealing out your wares
To all chance comers, at the village fair !
1000 I would come too, and claim you as my own :

To me you would be nobler far, dear Ann,
Selling your honest penn'orths openly
Thus in the street, and in your own poor dress,
Than some I know of, who are not ashamed
1005 To flirt and flutter through a gay bazaar
Vending kiss'd bouquets, all for charity."

She did not understand : how should she know
That *bouquet* means a posy, and that *vend*
Is much the same as selling?   So at once
1010 She said : " Ah winna do it, Master dear,
If yo can think it shaames yo ; but Ah know
It's *me* as shaames yo, if theer's owt to shaame!"

" You do not shame me, dear," her husband said ;
" No, nor your kindred, nor your meanest work.
1015 You should not think so, and you need not fear
That I shall ever think so.   Burlinghope
Knows me, and knows that you are now my wife ;
And that's enough."
                            " Aye, that's enoogh," she said ;
" The folks all know I are your servant still,
1020 And yo my Master : that's the best on it !"

" Well, we will tell them we are coming, then.
You shall go first, and stay with brother Jim,

And choose a cottage; mind, a pretty one;
A cottage with a garden and a view."

1025   "Aye, an' a yard!   Ah always like a yard,
For wood an' cawls; a yard wi' bricken floor,
An' room to stoomp aboot i' pattens in,
An' twirl a mop; an' it mun have a sink,
To save the kitchen, for my washin oop!"
1030 He raised his eyebrows: "Fair enthusiast!"
Said he, "your tastes are sound and practical,
Your requisitions just.   It will be joy,
To see you on your pattens in that yard,
Trundling your mop!   Of all domestic feats,
1035 I love to see the misty water rise,
Like a wet aureole, from the swiftspun mop
Twirl'd by a hearty woman, such as you,
Upon a round red rustic arm, like yours.
Therefore, *mia cara sposa*, take *carte blanche*,
1040 And have your wishes gratified."

                                           She stared;
And look'd at him with grave reproachful eyes:
"Master, Ah lay yo're makin' gaame o' me,
Wi' them fine words; an' it's too bad o' you!
Yo should speak jannock, to a simple wench
1045 As talks her own plain talk, an' has naw sense
To skill sich words as them!"

                                   "You're right, my lass,

And I was wrong. I love your country talk,
And when I hear it, something eggs me on
To grace it with a contrast and a foil,
1050 By using words as long as asses' ears,
Which pedants have invented. Never mind :
I only meant that you should have your wish—
A cottage with a yard."
                              " Aye Sir, that's it :
Owd Mary's cottage had a yard like that,
1055 An' her'll be dead by now : Ah'll ax oor Jim.
When mun Ah goo ? "
                              " To-morrow, if you like ;
The early train."
                              " Aye, but it's carrier's day :
He'll tak' me in his cart to Albany,
An' then Ah'll walk ; it inna far to Jim's."

1060 " Well—but your luggage ? "
                              " Looggage ? Bless your heart !
What do Ah want wi' looggage ?   Ah shall weer
A workin aapron, under ; an' for things—
Why, broosh an' cawmb ; stockins ; a shift or two ;
A neetgoon ; an' mah cotton bonnet ; theer—
1065 That's looggage !   Yan blew cotton handkercher
'Ull hold 'em all.   It inna mooch to loog,
For me, 'at's carried sacks ! "
                              " My dear," said he,

And vainly strove to hide his curious smile—
"All this is vulgar.   If my sister comes,
1070 Don't tell her how you travel ! "

                              " Eh, mah word !
Her Laadyship 'ull niver nawtice *me*,
Let alone speak.   But sure, at Burlinhope,
Yo winna want your sister ? "

                              " No, indeed !
Ann, *you* will have to be my sister there,
1075 And wife, and friends, and everything.   You see
How large your duty is."

                              " Aye, Sir, Ah see ! "
She said ; and sigh'd, and laid her glowing cheek
Against his knee : " Yo keep on sayin that,
To me, as knows na' moor o' folks like yourn,
1080 Nor if Ah was a baaby !   Ah do wish "
She added, looking fondly up at him,
" 'At Ah could be like all on 'em at onst ;
But yo mun learn me how."

                              " I will," he said,
And stroked her hair ; " You'll learn, at Burlinghope."

1085 She went : alone, and in the carrier's cart,
And with her bundle in the handkerchief.
She stay'd at brother Jim's ; and help'd them there,
Cleaning and cooking, feeding fowls and pigs ;

And fetching water from the village well,
1090 In that hood bonnet which she dearly loved,
Because he loved it ; and because the poor—
The labourers' wives, the servants, of the place,
Wore it, as she did.   And the neighbours came,
And saw her ring, and wonder'd that her hands
1095 Were still so rough, and she herself so plain
In dress and manners, talking as of old
Just as they all did : and at last, they said
"Why, Ann, your Master is a gentleman ;
"Yo've got to be a laady!"   "Have I, though?"
1100 Cried she, her blue eyes blazing out at them—
"Have I ?   Joost wait till Ah've got sattled, then,
An' yo shall see!   If he's a gentleman,
An' weds a workin wench, *that's* not to say
As wedlock turns him to a workin mon,
1105 Nor her into a laady!"
                                 Presently,
She took that cottage with the lovely yard ;
A cottage with a garden, and a view
That looks on Albany, and sees at night
The full moon risen over Elsley Mere.
1110 And then she wrote a letter ; it was this :—
"Dear Master, Jim have took it, what I said,
Owd Mary's cottage.   Her's bin dead an' gone
Too year this Crismas.   An' it's very nice ;

An' oh, the yard is butifull !   An' now
1115 I'll tell yo, I ha' clean'd it all mysel ;
    I've swep the floors an' scrubb'd 'em, an' the stares,
    And black'd the graats, an' done the witewashin,
    An' clean'd the paint ; an' Polly's a poor tool,
    But her an' me has paper'd all your room,
1120 Your parler, an' I hope yo'll like it, Sir,
    An' here's a bit, to show yo.   Me an' Jim
    Have done the gardin, an' theer's goosberies
    An' taters, an' I reckon it'll do,
    By what he say, till spring, or welly that ;
1125 An' then I'll dig it.   An' I think that's all ;
    An' Polly send her duty, likewise Jim ;
    An' me, I sends my love an' duty too,
    An' so no moor at presant, but I are
    Yor faithful wife an' lovin servant, Ann.
1130   P.S. Yo'll plese to send the furnicher,
    An' carpits.   I'll be redy for the men,
    An' I shall heeve the things an' put 'em strate,
    Yo may depend.   An' then, yo'll coom yoursell,
    That's best of all as cooms to me, my dear."

1135 How did it strike him, such a love-letter
    From such a wife ?   His far superior skill
    In letters, and the posture of his mind
    Toward learning and the arts ; the social force

That placed him where he was, and made him feel,
1140 What educated men should always feel
Toward ignorance : not hatred, not contempt,
But courteous condescension ; did not these
Cause him to wince at her endearing words
Misspelt and badly written ; and thereby
1145 Make him ashamed of his own love for her,
And of a love like hers ?

                   He certainly
Smiled, even laugh'd a little, as he read ;
But having read, he kiss'd the blotted page
And look'd at it intently, as he said
1150 "This letter is the outcome of herself :
Unconsciously pathetic !   Why, her words,
Her childish writing, her untutor'd phrase,
Her spelling—what are these, but evidence
That in her lie diviner purposes
1155 Than she can utter ; feelings more intense
Than she can put in words ; a character
Beyond mere words ?   It is the analogue
Of human souls ; which have within themselves
More than they know.   Her letter is a tale
1160 Of lowly woman's lowliest work ; obscure,
Uncouth, unsightly ; yet exalted far
Above the highest work that is not done
From motives such as hers.   She works for love ;

                                    D

A woman's love, that scorns to be repaid
1165 Except by love. All honour, all reward,
All public recognition of her name
As link'd with mine, are nothing : what she wants,
Her own poor labour gives her, in the joy
Of sacrifice, of self-abandonment,
1170 Of pure, devoted, unregarded toil
For him to whom she gives herself : for *me.*"

Strange, that a man like him should think and feel
So much, about a common servant maid !
Oh, singularly curious—if indeed
1175 In heart and in intelligence she were
What life and work had made her, otherwise.
But he had gauged her intellect aright ;
And, better still, had fructified her heart
Unwittingly, with such strong fortitude
1180 Of strenuous passion, as no insolence
From his class, and no rudeness from her own,
Could weaken or dissolve : her very soul
Was merged in his—the greater in the less :
For greatness still implies simplicity,
1185 And hers perforce was simpler far than his,
And had but one absorbing interest—Love.

He had his loftier work, his larger range

Of interests and enjoyments : and 'twas these
That help'd him most, to love her for herself
1190 And for her place ; because her place, her love,
Were so remotely different from his own.
His complex nature still included hers ;
He understood her simpleness ; he loved,
Just as it was, her homely womanhood,
1195 And cherish'd and adored it ; he rejoiced
To have her by him, in the peasant dress
That spoke her calling ; and he greatly cared
For the rough work to which she had been bred,
And for her hands that suffer'd it. To him,
1200 The pathos, the significance, of toil,
Express'd in hands like hers, were dearer far
Than jewell'd fingers jealously kept free
From all things that are common and unclean.

Thus then, renouncing fashion and the world,
1205 But not renouncing wisdom, nor the lore
Of ages, nor the books that treasure it,
Nor his own work, he went and dwelt with her
In that old cottage with the charming view,
That looks on Elsley Mere. He watch'd her there,
1210 Through circling seasons and through varying years,
With unabated interest, as she moved,
Cleaning the house, or in that lovely yard

Trundling her mop, or trotting to and fro
In pattens, with her bucket and her broom ;
1215 With love unfailing working on for him,
As he, were he a woman, would for her,
After her kind.

          But she above her kind
Rose bravely, help'd by him : she did not rise
In outward rank, in manners, nor in speech,
1220 Nor, least of all, in dress or finery ;
But of an evening, when she read to him
And ask'd him questions, or he read to her
And talk'd, his clear illuminating touch
Lit up the volume, till her fallow mind
1225 Received that nurture and retain'd it well.
So, step by step, in methods of his own,
He raised her ; till she gain'd a breadth of view
That took in all he wish'd ; and soon display'd
An active eager interest in mankind
1230 And this their dwelling place (too good for them,
Said he, if all the tales we hear be true)
That made her a companion for himself
Beyond all other women.   She was his ;
In mind and heart, his creature and her own ;
1235 But *they* were train'd elsewhere.   And presently,
He learnt, with wonder and a fond surprise,
How much she knew that he had never taught.

The country and its ways ; its birds and flowers,
Simples, sweet herbs ; the lore of moon and stars
1240 And lucky days ; and how soft rain water,
Dript from the aisins on Good Friday, keeps
Untainted for a twelvemonth. Things like these
She knew from childhood ; and her childhood now
Came back to her in womanhood : set free
1245 From all but Love's light service, she enjoy'd
Once more, her old employments and delights ;
The occupations of the field and farm,
And of her garden, and its fatted fowls.
These for the spring and summer ; and anon
1250 She glean'd in harvest, and she gather'd nuts
And blackberries, and from the autumn woods
Brought home large fuel for her winter's fire.
Each season bless'd her ; its reviving joys
Refresh'd her life, and kept it still in bloom.

1255   But what said all the folks at Burlinghope,
Her kindred and her friends ? At first, they mused
And gossipp'd freely over him and her :
Some said, that since he was a gentleman,
He owt to rise her ; others thought it strange
1260 That she had no ambition to be rose.
They reckon'd it poorspirited and mean
In her, to live as she did : " But," said they,

" Her inna fit to be a laady—theer !
That's why."

"Then, what for did he marry her ?
1265 Maybe, he did it for to save her waage,
An' get her work for nothin."

"*Him ?*   Not he !
He's getten oother servants at the Grange ;
Aye, an' her knows it ; her was one on 'em,
Afoor he wed her.   An' of coorse, her knows
1270 Her could be Missis, now : but they do say
He lets his sister live theer."

" Well, Ah says
An' sticks to it, 'at Ann's a character :
Wife to a gentleman, an' works like us !
But what, her's free an' jannock wi' us all ;
1275 Niver oopsided, not a bit set oop,
But nods an' speaks to ivery one, as plain
As when her lived a-whoam."

Such was their talk—
The better sort of women, and the men.
But when they saw her in the village street
1280 Clad in her servant's dress, yet side by side
With him she loved, or even arm in arm,
They said, He shaamed hissel to walk wi' her,
And it was shaameful, her to shaame him so !

And other women met her at the well,
1285 And spoke their minds : said Betsy from the farm,
"Ann, Ah do wonder thou can be so bold
To walk wi' him a-thatns ! Goodness me !
If Ah was married to a mon like that,
Ah wouldna slaave i' kitchen, saame as thee ;
1290 Ah'd let him know Ah was a laady, then !
Ah'd dress me oop, an' mak' him taake ma' oot
A-pleasurin, Ah would !"
                        Indignant Ann
Look'd full at Betsy, as she answer'd her :
"Aye, *that* thee would ! Ah could ha' tell'd thee that !
1295 But thou's not me : thou niver had a mon
To show thee what a bafflin thing it is
To be a laady. I ha' tried it, onst ;
An' coom what will, Ah winna try na moor."
So saying, she lift up her brimming pails,
1300 Poised on her yoke, and strode away ; erect,
And scornful, and majestic. Not a word
From those distracted women, reached her ears;
They could not understand her ; but they felt
That, though so like them in her work and dress,
1305 She was not of them : and they let her be.

For women cannot do without a sign :
Superior man may see himself revered

Without the help of trappings or of toys ;
Poor and untitled, in a peasant's garb,
1310 He rules his fellow men, and makes them feel
The force of manhood, simply as a man :
But rank, and power, and beauty well adorn'd,
And social skill, and daintiness of mien,
And sumptuous clothing—she who has not these
1315 May rise above her fellows, in repute—
In act—in character—in intellect ;
May be heroic, queenly, beautiful ;
Yet, having not the ensigns of a queen,
She cannot rule her sex, nor govern ours ;
1320 She has but little influence on men,
And none at all on women.   Is this hard ?
Well, there is one thing, one great thing alone,
That gives her power to rule, without the aid
Of any sign save Love ; a nobler rule
1325 Than Man can ever hope for.   It is this :
Religion, and her child Self-sacrifice.

Ann, moving homeward, stately and superb,
With heaving heart, between her balanced pails,
Thought not of these things.   No, she only thought
1330 That she would never tell him what they said,
Those foolish maids, about her : she would wait
And leave it all to Time ; slow silent Time,

Whose velvet step with slight recurring tread
Smooths out the footprints of Intolerance.
1335 She acted wisely ; in a few short months
All this had settled down.   The Master's name
Was had in honour ; Jim spoke up for him,
And Polly too ; and all the world could see
How well he loved his humble wife.   No doubt
1340 She was his servant, and his only one ;
But that was all *her* doings.   If she swept
And scrubb'd and clean'd, it was to please herself
And show her fondness in those simple ways
Most natural to her.   He honour'd her
1345 In public and in private ; and received
With courtesy her service and her love
As if she were a lady.   And for them,
Her neighbours, it was surely better far
That she was not a lady, and could live
1350 Among them as an equal.   Thus at last
They ceased to cavil at her working dress,
Or at her husband when he walk'd with her ;
Knowing she wore no other, save indeed
At church upon the Sundays, when she sat
1355 Beside him in her bettermost attire,
The simplest and the neatest woman there.
    Yet there were limits to her complaisance,
Even o' Sunday : gloves, and scents, and veils—

She still disdain'd such trumpery ; and he
1360 Disdain'd it too, for her.   Her working hands
Were always bare ; and, as they sat in church,
He fondly held her right hand in his own.

Such was their wedded life at Burlinghope :
Severe in its simplicity ; restrain'd
1365 Within the compass of a cottage home ;
And yet not mean, not vulgar.   He and she
Fulfill'd each other ; taking each the part
That Nature gave ; and she at least had scope
For all her powers.   Powers such as his
1370 Have small constraint of outward circumstance ;
All that they need, is leisure.
                                        As he look'd
Around him in the village, it was strange
To see his wife's position and his own
Respected everywhere, and yet not changed
1375 Each by the other.   He was not disgraced
Through marrying her ; nor she exalted much
By wedding him.   To all the villagers,
Women and men, it seem'd quite natural
That she should serve him ; and it seem'd but just
1380 That he should honour her, for doing so.
That was their verdict ; unexpress'd, but known
And acted on.   They all behaved to him

As if she were a lady ; and to her
As if her husband were a working man.
1385 No honour he could pay her, alter'd that ;
No sight of her, in peasant clothing clad,
Doing her day's work, lower'd in their eyes
Her husband's reputation.   And 'twas this
That most of all, delighted her : to be
1390 Just what she was, and yet, by being that,
Not to degrade him.

                           In her innocence
And meekness of behaviour, every day
She emphasized the contrast of her place
And his, by little tokens of respect
1395 And frank humility : to be call'd " Ann,"
"The Master's Ann," was joy to her ; and she,
She always call'd the village tradesmen " Sir,"
And curtsied to the parson ; and when friends
Came to her husband, she would show them in
1400 Just as a servant, to her husband's room,
And saying low " Ah'll fetch the Master, Sir,"
Respectfully retire.   Only in this
She show'd her wifehood : that she would remain,
If he were there and ask'd her to remain,
1405 Still in the parlour, with those friends of his ;
But merely as a quiet listener.
She would not talk : *he* liked her talk, indeed—

And it was something soften'd now, by his—
But her bad grammar and her country speech
1410 Would shock the strangers : No! she would not talk,
Nor yet be seated ; if she must sit down
And sit with him, they two should be alone.

That was her method ; and her steadfast will,
Obedient always to his lightest wish
1415 In things above her province, yet in this
Was obstinate ; no hints and no commands
Could change her scheme of conduct.   She was his ;
Wife, servant, everything ; and when she pleased,
Her own poor folk were welcome at the house,
1420 To see and hear her, and she talk'd with them
Freely before him ; for from him and them
She had no secrets.   But her constant heart
Was jealous of that outer world of his
In which he lived, and could not choose but live,
1425 Even now, when he and she were wholly one
And dwelt alone together.   What had she
To do with ladies or with gentlemen,
Save only him ?   And why should they, forsooth,
Come here a-traipsing, for to spy her out—
1430 Her lowliness, her ignorance, her love ?

Well, let them come, and she to do for them :
He would enjoy it, and 'twas right and fair
To see his friends at home, as she saw hers :

She need not mind their presence ; she was sure
1435 They could not come between her love and him ;
But oh, if he would be so very kind
As not to let them notice her !

                         "Ah think,"
She gravely said, "if yo'd be ruled by me
This onst, Ah could abear 'em, Master dear :
1440 Yo never tell 'em as I are your wife,
But let me bide i' kitchen, unbeknown,
An' fetch yoong Polly for to wait on 'em :
Her moother 'ud be thankful for the waage."

"Indeed ?" said he ; "but, Ann, it is too late :
1445 My friends already know you are my wife ;
Do you suppose that I would let them come
Without that knowledge ?"

                        "Well then, if they know,
Yo tell 'em not to notice me at all,
An' say, it's me as wishes it.   Oh dear !
1450 Ah'd do a servant's work wi' any one,
For all your friends ; but for to sit me down
Wi' gentlemen an' laadies, in a room,
An' talk, an' try to seem like one on 'em,
Why, it's ridic'lous, for a wench like me :
1455 I ax your pardon, but Ah mun say this ;
Ah winna do it, an' it's not my plaace !"